Leaving Ray

Janis Spehr

Leaving Ray

for my friends

Leaving Ray
ISBN 978 1 74027 882 9
Copyright © text Janis Spehr 2014
Cover photo © Ginninderra Press 2014

First published 2014
Reprinted 2016

GINNINDERRA PRESS
PO Box 3461 Port Adelaide 5015
www.ginninderrapress.com.au

Contents

Leaving Ray

When she wakes, it's still dark and the row of beads lie forest-cool against her skin. The man beside her sleeps solid as a fallen log. She eases herself out of bed, pulls on thick socks and pads to the kitchen. Everything's arranged: the dried dishes form neat ceramic humps along the sink and, when she opens the door, the fridge's delicatessen light shows a tub of margarine and the plastic containers of shredded lettuce, sliced tomato and processed ham. She works quickly, pressing white bread against vegetables and meat, sprinkling salt and pepper and adding a spicy pickle for James. Through the window, the bluish halo of dawn catches the metal spikes on the truck, the cradle for the logs. It's almost done.

She parcels the sandwiches in Gladwrap, stacks them in the fridge and stands at the window, her fingers on the beads. She wore these the day she was married, standing in the church listening to the minister's voice drone and feeling nauseous from the pressing weight of the child. They were the *something old* her fiancé laughed about as he slung them around her neck that morning. *Can't imagine you not wearing these.* For a moment she wanted to twist the thread and throw them away, those cheap glass beads strung in primary school and kept like a rosary all these years, but she just smiled and let him fasten the clasp. *I'm doing the right thing.* When Evan was born, she lay watching them cast rainbow shards against dim walls, the light strained by sentinel trees lancing her puerperal hours.

Her husband was always at work. Before the sun cleared the hills and while the rain trickled dismal streamers down glass, she heard him clanging wood into the stove and boiling water for tea. He loved these mornings, the grey sun ascending through dark branches and carving tracks through smoky drifts of air. The twenty-four wheels of the truck sounded like thunder and she would lie there, listening to them zigzag precariously down the road which joined the highway five kilometres below. Loggerdog. The sign sat proudly on the truck's nose. *I work like a dog.* He said this, cheerfully, all the time, while she, able only to coast above her body, languished for whole afternoons in a teenage summer.

Against a prickly tartan rug spread beneath criss-crossed branches, she and Sandra were just two country girls with bleached hair, cut-off jeans and sugary pink lipstick spread thickly as cream. She'd throw the beads so that they lay like flotsam beneath fetid water patterned with the slimy flux of eels then watch Sandra dive and break the surface with the glass spangling her hands. *Catch me, catch me now*, flashing naked through the scrub laughing as they pitched and wrestled the beads spilling clear light in silty dirt their fingers twined and scrabbling but Sandra broke free, always running ahead, out of that redneck town with its annual Truck and Country Music Show where the timber yards belched mucus-coloured smoke at midnight. There were letters from the Big Smoke – You'll love it, you'll love it here – but after a while they dried up like an empty creek bed running into dust. It was easy to sit behind the desk in the timber yard office typing and filing and watching the trucks come in. Easy to laugh in the right places when the men came in off shift jokey and eager to please Ray Brett Shane Glenn *don't listen to what this animal says.* She got crowned Miss AKD Softwoods 1975 with them making bets on whether she was a virgin and then Sandra came home from uni with Rebecca, walking down the main street with her hair razored to a stubble, her father's tears, her mother's screaming, and the town hissing delighted fountains of gossip *they're heartbroken…* Heart-broken: a stone split unevenly in two. Ray gave Miss Softwoods a heart-shaped, pink ceramic jewellery box and the beads lay at the bottom tangled with Brazilian coins and the hippie earrings her sister brought back from India. Ray brought around carnations and chocolates and a wristwatch with a heart-shaped gold face. The girls in the office cooed over the diamond which led to that slow walk down slightly scuffed crimson carpet the lovely lilies the week's honeymoon in Fiji and the four-year-old brick veneer high up in the hills but there was always the crackling counterpoint of Sandra *who comes from a normal family* parading down the street with Shelly then Elana then Fi, the names strung haphazardly as baubles on twine. A collision on a corner on Safeway one Friday afternoon, *hi, Deidre, how're you goin'*, acting as though she'd never been away, never worn a pinstriped vest and braces, never seen a doe rabbit dragging her soft belly on the ground caught in the headlights' glare.

The beads got fished from the garbage by Ray's mother, that child of Depression thrift, to *make a pretty toy for the baby*. She hung them over the cot with a plastic dolphin the morning Ray drove his wife to the hospital. *It's hard but wonderful* the girls in the office said but no one told her about being split like a watermelon, spread and screaming, stitched together again then falling into endless afternoons of viscous water and light while pyramids of dross built up behind doors and along windowsills and she woke in time to face her husband's bewildered homecoming questions. *You haven't done anything. Why haven't you done anything?*

When she stopped looking after the child, they took her to the doctor, who wrote out a prescription for happy pills and recommended the local hydrotherapy class. *Getting out with the other mums will do you good.* Evenings she sat in front of *LA Law* while Ray tinkered in his shed. When she lay beside him, she was often someone else; when she lay beneath him, she was always somewhere else, the stars glimpsed through the window promising another red wall of pain, but James slipped out easily as an eel, her luminous, wand-fingered boy grasping at the web of spinning lights. She walked him in a pusher along mountain tracks then came home to cook lunch and tidy up the rubble of toys, the miniature trucks which got larger and larger until the first boy started school. She cut lunches and ironed clothes and drove the Commodore, Mum's Taxi, a mundane diamond in the rear window.

Every February she spread a tartan rug for her family at the Truck and Country Music Festival, the gleaming wheels dwarfing her children as Evan ran shouting among the latest model utes and James helped the ladies set out cakes. *There's something wrong with that boy,* Ray said in a worried tone of voice. *You had him around at home too much.* Men in white sequinned suits often sang about the cold Kentucky rain and Slim Dusty walked a country mile around hay bales and Rotary hot dog stands. It was *a great day out,* everyone agreed, shovelling paper plates and plastic forks into bins. A great day a great day a great day, piling into the Holden station wagon, the four-wheel-drive, the rusty ute with its two yapping heelers but *gotta go home, get the kids off to school* and then driving through the town, the smoke from AKD, the braying cows in abattoir-bound trucks and the lake dark as an eye with its skim of foam.

Pouring milk into bowls set out on a chequered cloth while Loggerdog, that faithful plodding dog, toiled steadily up and down the hills and the radio babbled news of the Gulf War, the Barcelona Olympics, the information superhighway leading all the way to the local Harvey Norman and the Pentium 486 for the boys' assignments and things. *Learning is a lifelong process,* a teacher told Deidre at a parent–teacher night. *Learning is a thing which never ends.* Coming into Evan's room one evening with a load of clean footy gear, *learning should always be encouraged,* the smell of frying rissoles and boiling veg and on the screen a tumble of frozen flesh, a black snarling butch and a white and lacy femme. *Finish your homework, sweetie.* Deidre might have been blind for all the notice she took, but later she lay next to Ray thinking about those pliant silicon girls, that avalanche of thighs and hair. *Learning is a lifelong process. Learning is a thing which never ends.* This is what she remembered after Ray took the truck away and the school bus rumbled down the hill.

www.hotlezaction www.womanonwoman www.wetwomen The pictures splayed out before her eyes, that salmon-coloured skin, the hair bleached white as grass sliding beneath her fingers the kohl-rimmed eyes glowing black like holes in ice. Her finger traced a shaved runway of pubic hair, the screen dabbed with greasy moisture from her hand. The old chair creaked; she shifted and moaned, her heat locked on the kitchen vinyl. She gagged herself before that swell of bodies, she rocked back and forth, then the phone's shrill tore her hand away. (It was someone wanting money for the Heart Foundation.) The rest of the day she vacuumed and scrubbed, kneeling beside the bath like a penitent until her knees reddened and her fingers ached but it was no good and that night she crawled into bed beside Ray swollen and dirty as a leper, mounted and rode him to his amazed and grateful pleasure then next day she started all over again.

At the end of the month, Ray came into the kitchen, *jeez, look at this*, Internet bill in hand, eyes flapping concern but all Deidre said, looking him straight in the eye was *School, Ray, we have to educate our children.*

The kids went away on a school camp and she stayed up all night, huddled in a blanket in her son's room until thin bird voices cajoled her into the kitchen, where she plugged in the kettle like a zombie, her fingers trembling while the beads strung in the window clutched at the threadbare light.

But all good things blur to a bore: the same mouths the same eyes the tits cunt arse elbows everywhere, the same the same the same. *Can you talk to people on the Internet?* Deidre asked Evan one evening. *Talk to them about their hobbies and things? Oh, get with the program, Mum.* So Deidre voyaged out into cyberspace as longfingers who knew all about chatrooms and online dating. Longfingers could be anyone, go anywhere, a binary ballerina with a slippy slippy heart. She danced jadedly with Jade, serenaded Serena and bumped along the information autobahn with Anna-marie. One night she entered the 'Ladies Lounge', advertising all kinds of *lovelorn gay ladies seeking romance relationships and discreet bi-adventures.* Deidre scrolled expertly through a gallery of yearning and hope: *Rachael from Liverpool (NSW) breeds poodles and seeks genuine ladies only.* (Deidre had become considerably more sophisticated over the last few months and wondered if this was some warning to transsexuals.) *Sophie from Oxford sails through life like a Proustian beret* (better than being *in* a Proustian beret) and then there's Sandra, tanned face under a regal white crop *49 yo professor of archaeology survivor of recently ended 11 year relationship. Interests include films, baseball, jogging, camping. Seeks contact with professional woman (pref 35–55) for friendship poss rel/ship.* longfingers logs on: *a 43 yo doctor from Australia loves to travel. Pastimes: swimming camping bushwalking music, and often watch your wonderful national game on cable! Write me now!*

She does! Sandra and longfingers hit it off! Their messages arc across the ocean they're batted back and forth like strikes from highspeed pitches and Deidre hears all about Patti the real estate agent with the heart of solid tin, which type of expensive tents Sandra owns and the joys of white-water rafting… Sandra asks where the fascinating doctor goes. Longfingers vividly describes the Otways, that *dense and temperate rainforest*, the haunting canopies of leaves, the breathing soil, *fetid water patterned with the slimy flux of eels*, white splinters from a dropped strand of light…

silence

a number of silent weeks go by

(Loggerdog trawls bravely up the hills)

then

you left me

i didn't mean to

you liar   *betrayer*

i didn't mean to   *I was scared*

not good enough!

a number of furious weeks go by

you'd be surprised how the old place has changed

not changed enough

they no longer hold Miss AKD Softwoods

missed that   send me pictures of the tiara and gown

(an attachment of photos from 1975)

gorgeous thank god the seventies will never come again

perhaps you'd like to see how the kids look

no   anyway, they probably look like Ray

bitch   i missed you   all these years

suffer

i did

the ticket's at the airport.

Then all that's left is
suitcase
sandwiches
note

    She writes quickly and fluently. The sloping letters slash the page but she doesn't say sorry because she knows there's no forgiveness, no redemption for what she's doing, her sons splattered with the hot scald of gossip within the hour and the trail of whispers following her across the sea *they're heartbroken*. She thinks that her husband will be all right, that the truck will continue to toil methodically up and down the hills gallantly bearing its load of logs. In time he will meet a busy practical younger girl who will bear him two children and they will grow up to watch the trees fall in stately measure arcs. She hates the trees; they've fenced her life, thrusting their dark heads through drizzle and fog. She dreams of the desert, of snow-haired, leathery wise women squinting into the sun and of flattened-out red-dirt names drying her fertile body to a husk. Once she gets there, she'll send her boys a few seeds in an envelope, light enough to be strung on a single cotton thread, ephemera tossed on the wind or pounded to a floury paste. She flings a sheet of pink and lilac flowers across the table then sets down the plain white bowls, taking care not to clatter them against the knives.

She leaves the note weighted with the string of beads, those chipped and splintered orbs holding the history of two girls their heads pressed together in a primary school art class one February afternoon, the hot air pressed down with the weight of eucalyptus from the trees outside. *What will we do? Let's do this!* The beads carefully guarded against pillaging outsiders, strung then sliding onto the floor in a giggling fit, strung again, the ends of the string knotted and forced around the joining clasp. *I want them! No, I want them!* A bundle of legs against the old boards and fingers clamping floss-fine hair until a teacher in a flowered shift pulls them apart and tells them to *stop acting like boys! Deidre! Sandra!* Holding a pad of gauze over a knee grooved bloody and stroking a tender scratch. *You keep them! No, you keep them!* A sullen truce, the beads kept close by one, then surrendered, passed back and forth all year, adorning the Virgin Mary's blue gown in the Christmas play or swinging in the airy window of a summer cubby house. Worn to a first high school dance over a black nylon blouse and a burgundy hostess skirt, draped across the bass amp, the three gigs her brother's Glam Rock tribute band played and afterwards at a party one night, drunken stumbles on the dance floor, a haze of Jim Beam and joints making two chicks together OK. The drunken pash on frayed satin cushions, sharp animal wet-scent lading stale perfume, Santana's rhythm, a crazy giggling tumble into a car parked away from the light, wet-scent on fingers, snarling hair pillowed beneath her, the wet-scent of fingers kissed one by one, fingers slowly kissed then sucked then inside. Next morning a bruise delicate as a thumbprint on fruit next to her mouth and then the phone call *let's go to the creek*. They found each other in a small clearing, spreading the rug on the damp mulch of leaves next to the old Holden workhorse, solid with the beads dangling from its rear-view mirror. Later they bathed in the humid brown water and burnt leeches off their arms with a ten-cent plastic lighter, laughing and flinging the blood-gorged filth away. *We could go away and be always like this*, nestled together on the rug. *We could go away together* but already Ray was coming round to chop up half a shed of redgum and drive her to the cricket.

Ray's a good steady boy, her father said. *We could go away and get a flat*. Sandra's hand moulded a timid waist. *Ray's a good steady boy*, her mother said. *We could go away… Ray's a really top bloke*, her brother said. *We could go away a really top bloke we could go away a good steady boy a good steady boy we could go a good steady boy a really great mate a good steady boy we could…*

After she whispers the phone call, she moves quietly to the room where her youngest son lies in a naked tangle. She touches his face then the spiny dune of fur which runs from his navel to his nestled cock, straightens the sheet, pulls up the blankets, looks at her note… (*she shreds the note, she tears it to confetti then leaves it strewn in a careless spiral at the bottom of the bin. When Ray comes into the kitchen, she kisses him good morning and he gives a little skittish wince then switches the kettle on. The boys draggle in, yawning and scratching, jostling each other companionably and whingeing that she forgot to buy Coco-Pops. She shreds the note and her life runs on, driving them to footy training, working her one-day-a-week at Bi-Lo, then another Truck Show…*) but then there's a gravely crunch of tyres, the taxi's watery overhead light, as the door swings open. *Looks like a good day for it,* but she doesn't know him, a man with piebald stubble and a blurry mermaid along one arm. *Yes, a good day,* she echoes, a stroke of luck, no conversation needed about hubby and the kids, she'll make up stories, say she's bound for Ballarat for Tottenham for Rio de Janeiro, driving fifty kilometres a month ago so no one would see her fill the passport application out.

She carries a small handbag, wears a skirt and clumpy-heeled shoes because she knows what this town is like; can't let it be said that she left looking like *a freakshow her hair was pink, she wore six-inch stiletto heels, her vinyl dress patterned like a snake.* The dog twitches and stirs but he's too old to bother waking up the house. (She remembers him, a tiny spotted pup whining when Ray put him in the kennel the first night. *He has to learn to be on his own.*)

Static cleaves the news and weather, there's the spin of a gold-furred steering wheel and it's done, leaving behind her sling of safety, that net of comfort, for the promises of a postcard sun. The single light from the kitchen impales her regret but already it's cracking like the stains across an old, imperfectly sealed photograph. She remembers James learning to walk, catching him before he pitched and fell. She remembers Sandra, exile-eyes gazing straight ahead in the main street but not letting go her girlfriend's hand. *She had to learn to be on her own.* Her own life's been a pact, a refuge which was never sanctuary, but now impatience fires her veins and, as the taxi pulls into the station, she sees the first yellow tips of leaves shooting from woody stems. She feels unfurling blossom flame vital as capillaries through her body. She wants to be an honest pariah. She is going to join the other outlaws and, as she hands the man money and steps onto the moving train, her history refracts, splattering its neon harvest across the bridal thaw of her heart.

The Red Jumper

He was standing by the cash register when she came into the shop, a wiry little piece with blonde hair he doubted was natural. She looked all right, though; didn't have any rings through her nose or green plaits.

'You right there, are you? Anything I can help you with?'

And then there was her question about the jumper; the story about running out of petrol that morning and having to walk to the shop.

'Your wife sold me some, even though I didn't have any money.' She dropped a few coins into his hand.

He wasn't surprised. When he'd been out on the farm, he was always pulling bogged cars out of mud or towing the ones which had broken down. Even here, it happened; tourists staying in the big town up the road came out to look at the scenery and got into trouble. Annette would have sold her the petrol in an empty oil container they kept out the back – illegal because it was plastic. The girl would have been flustered, worried about leaving her car and not having any money. That's why she'd forgotten her jumper.

'I'll ask the wife,' and he went out the back, where Annette stood preparing chips. Skeins of peel curled like dirty ribbons in the sink. When he asked her about the jumper, her face went blank.

'No, I haven't seen it.'

'You sure? One of the girls might have…'

'No.' She looked at him patiently, the peeler clutched in her hand. 'She's got the wrong end of the stick. She must have left it somewhere else.'

'We haven't seen it, love,' and he watched the pretty face fall in disappointment.

'Oh, well, if you do…'

'Yeah, yeah,' he said, taking the piece of paper with the scribbled phone number.

He wanted her out of there; he could see Des the ambo coming along the footpath for a packet of smokes, his beanie pulled down over his ears.

Des held the door open for the little blonde and gave her the once over as she went through. 'G'day.'

'G'day, Des.' Automatically he reached for a packet of Peter Jackson and waited while Des ambled around collecting biscuits and dog food.

'Wish he wouldn't come here,' Annette had said, not long ago.

'He only lives around the corner. He's entitled,' he'd answered, but she was right; he felt the man's presence like a judgement. It didn't matter how many times Des came in for cigarettes and cans of Pal, he would always see him bent over Damien's body, big hands pressing down and his ear cocked for a sigh of breath. When he saw Des, he smelt dank water and saw green slime.

He gave the man his change and got Annette to take over while he sat in front of the television having his tea and refereeing his daughters. Shouts carried faintly from the oval down the road where the footy team trained under lights; he saw the night air stained white by young men's breath and veils of steam rising in the showers.

Later the blokes came tramping into the shop, calling out to him with flushed faces and slicked down hair.

'Hey, Graeme, how's it going, mate?'

They milled around, ordering drinks and greasy food, reminding him of the time he was their age and had done the same thing. In a few years…but he wouldn't let himself think about it. He shovelled chips into bags and piled slabs of meat onto hamburgers then cleaned up and switched out the lights.

The first thing he saw when he walked into the bedroom was the jumper draped like a flag across the old dresser. Bright red, just as the girl had described. Like the colour of geraniums when they first open.

Annette had once had a skirt the same colour, a silky thing which belled softly from her hips. She must have found the jumper when she was tidying up. He'd give the girl a call tomorrow. He piled his clothes neatly onto a chair and eased quietly into bed, even though he knew nothing could wake Annette once the drugs had kicked in. He lay there with his eyes open, listening to the dark.

The sounds were all different in town. He used to get up during the night, after his son died, and stand at the kitchen window, hearing the dry screaming of possums and the wind strumming the antenna on the roof. Under moonlight, the dam was a dark unblinking eye. Dawn always came as a surprise, that first metallic harshness unsoftened by sun and he'd stumble out to the old privy to have a piss and unchain the dogs. He'd get cranky with Annette in the dairy and sometimes, when she left to get the girls off to school, she wouldn't return. He'd come in for morning tea and she'd be at the sink, looking out the window, staring, staring at the dam.

He came in one morning to find her with the carving knife resting lazily against one wrist, from which oozed a dark glistening tear.

'A fresh start might do you the world of good,' said the doctor as he wrote out the prescription for the pills. 'Might be just what you need,' and then he told them about the old lady selling up in town.

'Well, it's just a spot on the highway,' Annette said when they went to look it over.

'Yep, just a spot on the highway,' he echoed, and in the end, that's what they called it.

People said that they were mad to buy the shop, that they wouldn't make a go of it, but they'd done all right. It was her idea to put the collection of old bottles and tins in the windows to get the tourists in, the tea tin with the kookaburra on it and the flat metal boxes which had once held cigarettes. He usually spun some bullshit about them all belonging to his grandfather but they were mainly old junk he'd found when he'd cleaned out the sheds on the farm, along with yellowing copies of the *Weekly Times* and rabbit carcasses hung up to dry years ago.

They painted the shop cream with dark green trim – 'heritage colours' Annette called them – and he got a signwriter to design a scroll above the door: 'Proprietors: Graeme and Annette Maxwell'. Annette had learned to make biscuits and fudge squares and rum balls, which she boxed and sold with gingham covers to the tourists.

He tried not to think about the farm but he missed it like a wound, especially in spring when the grass was beginning to kick and the calves lay neat as parcels at their mothers' feet. The dam was out of sight but he still carried Damien with him and at night dream-tentacles wrapped his sleep until he sweated and cried out. He flailed through black water but always his son lay out of reach, arms upturned like a sacrifice and hair a floating film of blonde weed. When his mouth opened to shout Damien's name, water rushed in and his nostrils clogged with dirt. He clutched at flesh and bone which dissolved into white ripples and floated away.

He woke with fragments of the dream still clinging and stumbled down the passage to sluice them off. When he came out of the bathroom, waist wrapped with a towel, Jayne was standing outside the girls' room, her arms overflowing with Princess, the big old tabby they'd kept from the farm.

'This cat smells like kitchens,' she announced gravely.

'Don't be stupid,' he said. 'A cat can't smell like a kitchen,' but later, as he spooned down cereal, he sniffed surreptitiously at the old cat's fur and caught bread and cinnamon and his daughter's own warm body scent.

He took the broom and stood outside, raising his head to the air like a dog as the chills lift from the street. The oak trees opposite filtered the rising sun; the chemist a few doors up and the butcher on the other side were getting ready for the day and soon there was a line of brooms going 'swish, swish' in the gentle light.

By the time he finished sweeping, he felt better. He turned the 'Closed' sign to 'Open' and went inside to have the rest of his breakfast.

Annette stood at the sink opening a litre carton of milk. She was wearing the red jumper.

For a moment, he just stood there. Annette had always been

a cuddly girl, was a lot larger than the little blonde and the jumper pulled tightly across her breasts.

'You said you couldn't find it,' he said at last.

'What?' She picked up the kettle and turned on the tap.

'You said you couldn't find it.'

'What are you talking about? Oh, this.' She plucked at the jumper. 'She left it behind yesterday.'

'You told me you didn't know where it was.'

'So?' She looked at him as though he was stupid, turned the tap off and plugged the kettle in. Drops of water beaded the stainless steel then thinned into rivulets down its sides.

'But it's not yours! It doesn't even fit you!'

'It'll stretch,' she said and tugged complacently at the wool.

'What if she comes back and sees you wearing it?'

'She won't – she was a tourist. She started going on about how "quaint" the bottles were. I had to shut her up.'

'I've got her number. I could ring her.'

'Suit yourself.' She shrugged and turned away. 'I'm going to make toast. Do you want one slice or two?'

They had breakfast in silence then she took the car off somewhere while he went into the shop and started stacking shelves. It was a job which always bored him and ordinarily he tried to make a game of it, grouping tins of a certain size or colour on the floor then ranging up and down the aisles placing them where they were meant to go, but this morning his legs stayed weighted to the floor. He stood stolidly bending and stacking until the bell on the door clanged and Des came in for his paper. The bloke looked seedy. Des lived alone, didn't have any company except for his greyhounds and a couple of ferrets. While he was in the ambo's uniform he looked all right but today he wore old corduroy pants and gave off a sour smell, like mud drying in the sun. Under the fluorescent light his nose was purple as a baboon's arse.

'I was out at your old place yesterd'y. The wife gets asthma. The grass is up over the fence.'

'Yeah?'

They'd sold the place to a TAFE college professor and his wife who wanted to run a few horses. When he showed them around, he could see the wife doing sums in her head, adding up the cost of remodelling the kitchen and putting in a new bathroom. He wasn't surprised to hear that they'd let things go. He'd thought that they'd probably tear the old weatherboard down and build some ugly brick thing big as a spaceship with a flat easy-care native garden.

He stuffed a packet of cheese slices, cigarettes and a copy of *Post* into a plastic bag and handed it to Des, who grunted and looked at him shyly.

'I seen your missus take off this morning like a bat outta hell.'

'Yeah, she's busy.' He turned back to the shelves, trying to work out where to put some tins of condensed milk then glanced up to see the man's small grey eyes glazed with pity. *Get out*, he thought, feeling stripped and flayed. *Get out*, ripping the top from the carton and not looking up until he heard the bell clang.

He tore the box open and wondered where Annette was. She'd got into a habit of going off like this and he didn't feel he could ask her about it. There was a certain privacy she'd always had, that he never felt he could impose upon. The skirt she'd owned, the colour of dying autumn leaves…she'd worn it when they first started going together. He'd pick her up in his father's old Holden which usually sat in the shed and they'd drive to the beach, taking the back roads because he was still too young for a licence. They could go a whole afternoon without seeing anyone, just sitting on top of the cliffs watching the sea change colour under the sky or walking along the beach with the fierce tug of water around their ankles. When they first started doing it, they used the Holden's back seat but after a while they got braver and would spread a rug on the harsh tussocky grass which covered the dunes. One evening after they'd finished, they'd walked along the beach and come to a place where the ocean had sucked out a scoop of sand and left a trench of water behind, through which fronds of seaweed waved. It was almost dark when Annette handed him her shirt and stepped into the pool.

'What are you doing?' he'd asked, half-frightened, because this wasn't like her, but she just stood there with the darkness brushing her shoulders and the skirt spread and gently floating.

'Hey, come out of there!' He'd started to wade in but stopped when she held up her hand and it seemed now, as he knelt dazedly among the tins, that he'd caught a glimpse of something buried deep which would either flower or spoil.

He'd waited until she stepped from the water. The warm air dried the skirt and left a salty stain along the hem. He wondered what had happened to it, whether it lay at the bottom of one of the boxes they'd never bothered to unpack or whether Annette had sent it to the Salvos long ago. As they drove back from the beach that evening, with the Holden's headlights picking out startled rabbits on the road, he hadn't know what to say. Perhaps if he had she wouldn't be sinking into bottomless sleep and he wouldn't be spending his nights sifting bones and silt.

bones

and

silt

His son was just bones and silt now.

When he heard the car pull up, he looked out the window, thinking it must be Annette, but it wasn't the station wagon, just some Jap tin can with a dented fender.

The blonde girl got out and he gripped the shelf. She stared both ways along the street and for a moment he thought she was going somewhere else but then she looked through the window straight at him. The chemist's black and white border collie bounded up and she laughed and put out her hand. Now he remembered; she'd said she'd be back – 'just in case it turns up' – when he'd pushed her out the door. It seemed he forgot a lot of things these days – the correct way to put stock on shelves or where a lost garment might be found. She waved to him as she started across and he drew back his lips like a cornered animal. His mouth opened to form words of promise or denial but the sounds snagged and eddied in his chest and, as she came towards him, he smelt the stench of floating carrion and felt the water close over his head.

Learning the Alphabet

'You leave that poor little girl alone, Tom!' Mrs Murphy called to Grace's father across the Ladies Lounge. 'Stop torturing her!'

'He thinks we're corruptin' her,' said Dulcie, the big, dark woman, and there was a burst of laughter from the women at the table.

Grace's father tightened his grip on her hand. 'C'mon, Gracie,' he said.

'I was watching, watching the ladies.' Grace pointed.

Her mother had sent her into the public bar where her father was drinking with Mr Anderson. They had their hats pushed back and a half-empty packet of Cravens lay on the bar between them.

'Come on, Dad,' she'd said, tugging at his elbow. 'Mum's ready to go home.'

'Is she, Gracie? Well, you go on out. I won't be long,' but on her way out Grace had stopped to watch Mrs Murphy and her friends laughing and drinking and having the time of their lives.

Now Mrs Murphy smiled at her, blew out an 'O' of smoke, then looked at Grace's father. 'Well, go on, Tom. Be a shame to keep the lovely Maureen waiting,' and there was more laughter that gusted towards Grace like hot wind fanning fire.

'Ladies,' muttered her father, as he pushed open the door to the street. 'Yeah, that's a good one.'

Grace's mother stood on the footpath, wearing her full-skirted dress patterned with yellow and blue flowers. She carried a white handbag, which matched her shoes and looked, Grace thought, very pretty. 'You took your time.'

'I got held up.'

'Oh, held up, held up. The only holding up going on would be you and Kev holding up the bar.'

'Just be quiet, will you.' Grace's father started down the street to where the car was parked.

'Give me the keys, Tom.'

He looked at her for a moment. The brilliantine he always put on to go into town had set his hair into hard little waves. He handed her the keys.

Grace curled up in the back and didn't say anything. She hated it when it was like this. She wanted to be at home, sitting in front of her blackboard, making the letters she was learning in school. She watched the paddocks go by and saw the swamp with the dead trees sticking out of it like rotten old teeth. A tall white bird stood with its head down, fishing. Something startled it and it took off, a slanting white curve over grey water.

It must have reminded Grace's father, because he turned around holding out the feather to her. 'Hey, Gracie, look what I found in the paddock this morning.'

It was a parrot feather. Red and blue and green. Beautiful. Sometimes kids would bring feathers for Show and Tell but they were always black and white or black and blue.

'Give it here, Dad.' Grace stretched out her hand but her father held it out of reach, a teasing grin on his face.

'What do you say, Grace?' This was her mother, from behind the steering wheel, with her eyes fixed on the road.

'Please, Dad.'

'Uh-uh,' said her father. 'You have to be careful with this feather. It's a magic feather. It's a writing feather,' and he began to draw big letters on Grace's front. 'Well, here's a g, then there's an r, then an a, c, and e and that spells…'

'Grace!' yelled Grace, at the top of her voice.

'Shhh, Grace,' said her mother, but she was smiling, which meant she was over her bad mood.

'Please, Dad.' Grace held out her hand for the feather but her father was putting it away.

'I'll give it to you tomorrow, Gracie. If you're a good girl and help Mum with the dishes.'

'Promise?'

'Promise.'

They were almost home when a big shiny Ford with patches of rust showing like scars went past, travelling too fast and too close. Grace saw Dulcie and another woman who had been at the pub. It wasn't Mrs Murphy; she lived in town.

'No-hopers,' said her father.

'Going back to the blacks' camp,' said her mother.

'The blacks' camp,' chanted Grace softly under her breath. 'The blacks' camp, the blacks' camp.'

Next morning, Grace took the feather for Show and Tell and everyone admired it and said how pretty it was. Everyone except Steven Anderson.

'Your feather's piss weak,' he said at morning recess. 'Piss weak.'

'Is not,' said Grace. She didn't like him. He liked to walk past the girls when they were swinging from the parallel bars and yell out, 'Smelly snatch! Smelly snatch!'

'Is not,' mimicked Steven Anderson in a falsetto voice. He made a grab for the feather but Grace backed away.

'I'll tell my dad on you.'

'Your dad,' scoffed Steven Anderson. 'My dad says your dad keeps going in the wrong paddock.'

'You're dumb.' Grace knew there was something she didn't understand but she wasn't letting on. 'Your dad did not say that.'

'Did so. I heard him talking to my mum. He said, "Tom's going to get his dick caught in the barbed wire if he's not careful."'

Grace felt the ground shift slightly beneath her feet. The sun had been beating down all morning and had softened the asphalt where they played rounders and skippy. She smelt the sticky burning smell and heard the hot angry sound of the bees as they went about their business.

'Dick is a bad word,' she said at last.

'Dick, dick, dick!' shouted Steven Anderson. 'Dick, dick, dick!'

He made another dive for the feather but Grace was already running across the yard.

'Dick, dick, dick!' shouted Steven Anderson. 'He'll get his dick caught!'

Grace thought for the rest of the day about what he had said. It was on her mind even during the writing lesson when she copied out the fat, swelling 'a' and the 'r' crouched on the line as though waiting for the starter's gun. She thought about it on the way home as she walked along the hot and melting road with the three Fredericks kids from the farm next door. She left the feather on the mantelpiece; she didn't really want it any more.

'Dick is a bad word, isn't it, Mum?'

'Who's been telling you these words, Grace?' Her mother stood at the sink, up to her elbows in soapy water.

'Steven Anderson. He was saying things…he was saying things about Dad.'

'What things, Grace?'

'He said…' but Grace felt as though there was a net inside her chest drawn tight across the words. 'He said Dad keeps going in the wrong paddock,' she muttered miserably, looking down at her tea towel.

Her mother pressed her lips together and looked out the window. 'Don't worry about what people say, Grace. Things like that…aren't important.' She lifted her hands from the sink. The water had stained her skin scarlet and she looked as though she was wearing a pair of red, shiny gloves.

Grace's father came in, ready for his afternoon tea. He saw the feather lying on the mantelpiece. 'Hey, Gracie, don't you want your feather?' He began drawing a big 'g' on Grace's front.

'Don't, Dad.'

'Come on, Grace.' He made an 'i'.

'Oh, leave her alone, Tom, for God's sake!' snapped her mother.

Grace forgot all about the feather until next week, when she and her mother were in town again.

'Go on, you go in and get your father,' her mother said. 'Go on, off you go,' and Grace crossed the street and pushed open the door of the public bar.

It was dark in there and the air had a ripe, sour smell like old, rained-on grass. She couldn't see her father so she went through the door into the lounge.

'Who you lookin' for, love?' Dulcie sat at the corner table next to the cigarette machine.

There were a couple of other women there; one of them got up and wandered over to the jukebox.

'I'm looking for Dad,' Grace said.

'Who's Dad? Oh, Tom.' Dulcie blew out smoke. 'Well, he's not here. You could try looking out the back. He might be there.'

'Thank you,' said Grace politely. She turned towards the metal mesh door which led to the yard behind the pub.

'Met him on a Monday and my heart went boom,' sang the Chiffons behind her.

When she pushed open the door, she saw her father and Mrs Murphy. They were standing facing each other and her father had the feather! Grace stood at the top of the steps which led down to the yard and watched as he trailed it slowly down Mrs Murphy's throat, circled around the little hollow at the base and then gently stroked the V-shaped patch of skin at the opening of her dress. Mrs Murphy stood with her eyes closed and her head tilted back, as though she was listening for something she couldn't quite hear. Her lips moved but Grace couldn't make out what she was saying. Her father moved the feather – Grace giggled to herself – across Mrs Murphy's boobies. He was making a word! He drew the letter which looked like the ibis flying over the swamp, the one with the small neat head unfurling into the long sloping body and the little line which crossed it like a wing. Then the small cup-shaped letter which looked like a soft scoop of ice cream followed by the rounded letter with the gasping gap of a mouth. Before he could start on the next letter, Mrs Murphy knocked his hand away. She said something angrily, then looked up and saw Grace.

'Gracie!' Her father smiled and came towards her, feather in hand. 'You come to take me home?'

'Mum's waiting.' Grace stood on the step and watched Mrs Murphy do up the top button of her dress.

'Is she now?' Her father came up the steps and swung Grace onto his hip. 'Well, let's go and find her, eh?'

They went out through the lounge. Dulcie watched them pass and gave Grace a little smile. Grace didn't smile back; she was thinking about the feather and the letters. Thinking hard.

'I want ice cream, Dad,' she said, as soon as they were in the car.

'It makes you sick, Grace,' frowned her mother. 'Anyway, we haven't got time.'

'Please, Dad. I want ice cream.' Grace stared at her father.

He looked back, then put the feather, which had become damp and straggly in his hand, on the dashboard. He grinned. 'Yeah, righto, Grace. We'll get you some ice cream.' He slapped Grace lightly on her bare leg and put the car into gear.

On the way home they stopped off at the milk bar and Grace had ice cream. She had ice cream and a bag of lollies and a can of fizzy drink and strap of black liquorice. Everything she asked for, her father bought her.

'You'll be sick,' her mother kept saying but Grace didn't listen. She knew she wouldn't get sick. She felt full and happy.

'You had enough, Gracie?' called her father over his shoulder.

'Yes,' said Grace sleepily.

'That's good. You be a good girl now and we'll be home soon.'

They drove past the paddocks and the swamp with the drowned trees. Grace heard her parents talking but she was sleepy and her eyes kept closing.

'Bring in the groceries, Tom,' said her mother when they got home. She went inside to change.

'Yes, boss,' said Grace's father. But instead of going around to open the boot he picked up the feather. 'Come on, Grace. Come and sit next to me.'

'Why, Dad?' Grace was grumpy and felt sticky from all the sugar.

'Come on.' Her father patted the seat next to him, so Grace sat up groggily, opened the door and climbed in beside him.

'How are you going?' Her father ran the feather under Grace's chin.

'Good, Dad.'

'That's good,' said her father and he ran the feather light up the inside of her leg.

'That tickles, Dad!'

'Does it?' He ran the feather up her other leg and Grace screamed with laughter.

'Stop it, Dad! That tickles!'

But her father didn't stop. He ran the feather right up past her knee, almost to her fanny, then back down again, then up and down, faster and faster. It was tickling so much Grace couldn't stand it.

'Stop it, Dad, stop!' She tried to wriggle away but her father put out his other hand and held her.

'You're my good girl, aren't you, Gracie?' He wasn't tickling so hard now.

'Yes, Dad.'

'Promise? Promise to be my good girl?' He ran the feather lightly up her leg.

'Yes, Dad.'

'That's good,' said her father, still smiling. He put the feather away. 'That's good.'

On the way to school the next morning, Grace sat beside her mother on the front seat and watched the big blue car with the flaking patches of rust tear past, travelling towards town.

'Sluts,' said her mother, looking into the rear-view mirror, 'bloody sluts,' and her mouth was full of the hissing 's-s-s' sound.

It made Grace think of the snakes her father caught and killed in summer. He would break their backs with the shovel head then fling them over the fence so that the carcasses hung on the barbed wire, stiffening and blackening under the sun. Eventually they shrivelled up and dropped onto the ground but before this Grace had seen the small, flat eyes and the tongues flicking, venomous and deadly.

The Meeting

'Jesus died for somebody's sins but not mine…' Patti Smith

The girl stands in front of the mirror, tugging down the thin jumper. It's brown with white stripes and she knows it's no good. She has big saggy tits which drag the strips down and make them pucker and curve. She stands there, makes a face in the mirror then goes into the kitchen, where her father sits with the paper in front of the unlit wood stove.

So what's it gunna be like, this meeting?

I don't know, just a meeting.

There gunna be people there jumpin up and down, shoutin *praise de lawd?*

I don't know, says the girl.

Don't know, don't know. What do ya know?

Not a lot, says the girl and she walks down the front path, past rows of beans and cabbages neat as braided hair.

While she waits, she thinks about the half-dark hall, all the singing and crying and calling out to Jesus. (*Jesus ain't no lover for a woman.*) The caterwauling and bawling and upturned faces. Eva Pearson rolling on the floor with her dress pulled up under the pastor's moon-faced gaze.

The girl tugs down her jumper and listens for the car. The boy's late but she knows he'll turn up; they've had this arranged for a week. There's a sound like distant thunder and when the old puke-green Ford with the foxtail hanging from its antenna comes round the corner she grips the top of the gate so tightly flakes of rust come away in her hands. He's got a half-bottle of Jim Beam and when she hands it back the neck's ringed with brown smudges and sweat. She's seen him driving down the main street on Friday night, one hand on the steering wheel and the other on the can between his legs. She doesn't know why he comes to the meetings; she only knows that when they saw Eva Pearson on the floor their eyes met and he smirked. After the meeting, they sat out in the car while people called out cheerfully, you behave yourselves now, before going back to conversations about the Holy Spirit and the price of fencing wire. He kept looking at his hands and shifting around in his seat while she asked him about the footy team and how many wins they'd had. Not many, they were playing shithouse, and then he apologised for using language. He had a sweet face and smelt of Brut 33 and yes, she thought, he'll do.

At home, she brought up his family's name, just casually, and her father put down his paper and stared.

You going round with those tall Irish boys? You better watch yourself, girl.

The girl watched herself: she watched herself in the mirror and in the meetings and afterwards in the car. She sat on the hard wooden seats in the hall watching people open their mouths and utter dark streams of words which rose up to Jesus and wondered what it was like.

When he stops the car in the clearing, he hands her the bottle again but she shakes her head. She doesn't want to be like the girls she reads about in *Truth*: 'He drugged me then took advantage…' or 'Girl, sixteen, sold into degradation'. He leans towards her and she cups the hot mystery of his breath in her mouth, tastes liquor and smells cheap aftershave. When he tips the seat back, she knows he's done this before and she's glad. Their voices rise grappling and calling, past the dark trees, while she straddles him awkwardly and he fumbles with his zipper and swears. She expects pain but there isn't any and as she rides him her power rises like sap. Wild hallelujahs burst from her throat while he puts his hands on those heavy tits and moans as if he's receiving a sacrament or a blow. He's saying words she can't hear, begging slow down, slow down but he doesn't know she's got a dervish inside. Scarlet arpeggios leap from her and she opens to him like a flower, like a Venus flytrap while he howls in adoration below. She milks him and drinks him, tasting his sweet blood while his eyes roll back in his head and he clamours to be saved. He's moaning, he's begging, there's a sea of fire around them and when he cries ohchristgodjesus she blesses him and they glide, clear-eyed and sanctified, through to the other side.

On the way back, she tries to talk but he won't look at her. He only grunts and drops her at the corner instead of driving right up to the gate. The girl feels a flash of contempt but it passes and when she gets out she thanks him and gently closes the door. Branded, she thinks, watching the red gimlet eyes recede. The devil's spawn. The empty bottle hits the road and explodes into fragments of light. She starts walking.

When she reaches the house, she creeps in so she doesn't wake the others. The sky's clear and night light burnishes the old wood and worn lino. The girl takes down the big white enamel bowl with the dark blue rim, fills it from the kitchen tap and gets a thin rough towel from the cupboard in the hallway. She stands over the bowl and laves herself, ladling cool water between her thighs while she watches the tendrils of blood curl in the bowl and disappear. After she washes away the blood and stink, she dries herself with the towel, rubs herself so hard the skin mottles and streaks. She picks up the heavy bowl, carries it carefully to the yard and tips red-tinged water onto the plants. Then she goes inside and rinses and dries the bowl.

Still holding the towel, she moves quietly down the hall, and stands outside her brothers' room. Now you be a mother to them, her mother had whispered in the hospital but the girl didn't need to be told. She tiptoes in and strokes the hair of the littlest. They remind her of something she's seen in the window of the second-hand shop in town, the row of rotund wooden dolls with painted cheeks, which fit snugly, one inside the other.

When she reaches her room, she turns down the blankets and crawls under. Faint blue bruises bloom across her breasts; she feels a familiar soreness and knows that soon she will bleed. No drama, she thinks. In the morning she'll be up with the sun to get the boys off to school and will watch the bus raise the plumes of dust as it ambles along the road.

Her father will come into the kitchen wanting bacon and eggs and start yakking about the meeting. Who fell over? Go on, you tell me. Did that silly old bugger Jackie Merton fall over?

The girl sighs but then the lines on her face ease: no use wishing for something you don't have. Through the uncurtained window, she sees stars and the dense familiar outline of trees. She falls asleep beneath the dark mantle of sky.

Little Miss Tiny Tots

All down the highway Audrey, kept wanting to change her dress. She just wouldn't shut up.

He sat behind the wheel trying to blank her voice as the grey kilometres scrolled by but in the end he gave in. 'Yeah, all right, we'll stop soon and you can have a look for it.'

The pink travelling case containing her clothes and cosmetics had been packed in a flurry; her shoes had been thrown in on top of everything and then the zip jammed. He hoped she wouldn't find something missing and start making a scene. He would like to have gone a bit further, to have put some more distance between them and the lines of familiar houses, but he knew what she was like when she got going and, anyway, the sun had come out and pretty soon they'd start to bake in this shitbox that didn't have proper aircon.

'When are we going to stop? I want to pee!'

'Yeah, we'll stop soon, sweetheart, just over the top of this next hill.'

He remembered this town, remembered coming here years ago to see his mate Baz, who'd just set up a panel beating business. He remembered the trees big as houses down the grassy avenue dividing the main street, him and Baz hanging wheelies underneath the clock tower after midnight with two giggling chicks they'd picked up at the Continental Hotel. One had pissed off home but later he and Baz had gone through her friend on the back seat. Young blokes' stuff. Now he had the sun belting through the windscreen and Audrey jabbering in his ear and it was with relief that he crested the hill and saw the squat brown toilet block ahead.

He pulled over, got out and opened the door. 'You wait for me, Princess,' but she was already running ahead so he had no choice but to follow her into the entrance marked 'Ladies'. He fumbled in the pink case for the braid-trimmed dress then bent down to help Audrey pulled it on but his fingers stumbled over the unfamiliar fastenings.

'I can do it!' She turned irritably away and closed the small pearl buttons herself.

She hadn't had enough sleep; neither had he. All week, lying awake in the dingy flat, his scheme had festered like an open sore: if he could just distract Helen for long enough and if Big Connie wasn't there... He'd dragged himself through work and been told off twice by the manager. It didn't matter, though, because in the end everything had gone according to plan.

'We're going on an adventure, Princess,' he told her when they finally got away and she had seemed pleased enough, drumming her heels excitedly against the car seat as they drove through the petrochem plants and out through the western suburbs.

Now, standing the graffiti-splattered toilet, in front of a perspex mirror which gave back their streaky and imperfect images, she didn't seem so sure. 'I want plaits, Dad! And I'm hungry!'

'You only had breakfast a few minutes ago,' he joked.

'I want McDonalds!'

'I don't think there's McDonalds here, sweetheart. How about fish and chips?'

He couldn't manage the plaits. The blonde hair kept slipping though his fingers. In the end he gave up and just brushed it out until it lay in a glimmery sheen on her shoulders. He didn't know where it came from: no one in his family had snowy hair like that and when Helen had named her after the famous movie star they had both expected a little brunette stunner.

'You're beautiful, baby. You're my girl.'

As they drove further into the town, he tried to remember where Baz's business had been but it was ten years ago, more... Here and there, vacant shopfronts gaped emptily but there were cars everywhere and the streets seemed clogged with people. He had to wait a while in the fish and chips shop but when he finally placed his order he asked the guy behind the counter about Baz.

'No, mate, never heard of him.'

He turned back to his fryer, a big bloke running to fat, with time-blurred tattoos on both arms. *Judy: True Love Never Dies* was wrapped around a naked woman and a flaming heart. Oh, yeah. He could tell the fish and chip guy a few things about that – but probably nothing he didn't already know. Still, this imagined sense of kinship made for conversation.

'Seem to be a few people around today, mate.'

The guy grunted and heaved the glistening mound of chips onto paper. 'It's the show.'

'The show?'

'The *agricultural* show.'

'Oh, right.' Rednecks standing around looking at cows. Fat old women judging scones. 'Is there anything for little girls?'

'Whaddya mean?' The guy gave him a strange look.

'You know, a parade…' He floundered around, looking for the right word. 'A beauty contest… It's for my daughter.'

'Yeah, I think there's something like that.' The guy gave an indifferent shrug and drained the two pieces of flake. He turned the fish onto the chips and poured a shower of salt over everything. 'How old's your kid?'

'Just four. That's her there.' As he put money for the food on the counter, he showed the photo in his wallet.

'Oh, yeah. She's gunna be a real little heartbreaker in a few years.'

'She already is!' Impossible to tell the guy about the overflowing billow of love around his heart the first time he held her. He hadn't minded getting up at three a.m. when she cried. The first little tutu she had owned for her contests, when she was just a little tacker and could barely stand up, he had it in a box in the flat somewhere. He hurried out to the car, carrying the paper-wrapped parcel. 'I think I've got something for you, Princess.'

The guy in the shop had given directions and pretty soon he saw the red and yellow seats of the Ferris wheel, hanging in the air like stranded boats. There was a merry-go-round with about ten horses and a single row of sideshow clowns turned painted eyes first one way, then the other. Show jumpers stood in the centre of the arena, monumental haunches gleaming above steaming piles of shit. Through the open door of a corrugated iron shed he glimpsed tiered cakes, pavilioned and curlicued with icing.

'Come on, baby.'

There it was, a rickety wooden platform and a wooden shack with seats, behind it. A hand-painted sign read, 'Little Miss Tiny Tots', except some wag had tried scratching out the 'o' and replacing it with an 'i'.

'Is it too late, too late to enter?'

'No, you're right,' smiled the big woman with JUDGE pinned to her chest. 'There's plenty of room for the little girl to change over there.' She pointed to another toilet block but he'd had enough of that for one day.

Hurriedly, he unpacked the travelling case from the car. It had taken only a moment, in Audrey's room, to fold up the white tutu with its spangled fairy wings, to stuff in the satin slippers and the spangled headband and then to sneak the whole lot out to the car. Stuff Helen, the maggot-eaten, power-hungry bitch, always going on about her rights. No one ever gave a shit about his rights. He'd turn a day into a long weekend: he and Audrey would have a ball! The tutu was a bit crushed but he managed to fluff it out. He did his best with her hair, although any other time Helen would have done it up in big ice-cream curls.

He smoothed on a little bit of pink lipstick and touched the mascara wand to her lashes. 'You go and clean them up, sweetheart.' He gave her a little push and stood up to survey the competition as she trotted off.

There were half a dozen others, mainly done up in dresses, although one dark-skinned, dark-eyed, woggy-looking kid wore some kind of body stocking brightly patterned in red, green and yellow. All the girls wore make-up, although one of the mothers had overdone it and plastered a freckle-faced moppet with glitter and blue pools of grease. He felt uncomfortable looking at her, a five-year-old with a whore's mouth and come-fuck-me eyes.

'All get in a line, please, girls!' The judge made them all stand facing her, looking from the makeshift stage.

Audrey was on one end of the line, face flushed and one hand kneading the stiff folds of tulle.

'Smile, Princess,' he called, which drew a dark look from the old bitch.

'Now please walk around for me, girls.'

Audrey put her hands up in the air and did a little twirly turn, like a ballerina. The judge smiled and wrote something down on the notepad in her hand.

The contests had been Helen's idea. She had entered Audrey in one at the local shopping mall. By the end of the year there had been a whole shelf of cups and trophies; by the time Audrey was three, they had had to buy a special cabinet to hold them.

'Sugar and spice and all things nice,' Helen used to chant, as she helped Audrey pull on the white tutu or the pink tutu or the mauve tutu and brushed the shining hair. 'Oh, Aud-drey…'

He'd back the four-wheel drive out of the garage and sound the horn. They'd walk down the path towards him, Helen wearing a dress or dark suit, not jeans and trainers like most of the other mums. She'd lead Audrey by the hand, shepherding her to the car and fastening the seat belt of the front passenger seat securely around her.

'And where would Miss Audrey like to go?' he'd ask, trying to sound like a Pommy chauffeur from an old movie and making her giggle and Helen laugh.

They'd been a team, the whole three of them, until Helen started bringing Big Connie's advice home from work.

'Connie thinks I have low self-esteem… Connie and I are going to a personal growth seminar this weekend…'

Personal growth! Wankers making money. They'd led Helen so far up the garden path it had turned into a one-way street.

'I need some time by myself.'

'Well, if you need so much time by yourself, I'll take Audrey.' But it turned out this wasn't what was meant. Helen should have been here; she would have taken charge and charmed the judge who was draping the blue sash over the woggy-looking kid in the body stocking. Second went to a redhead in a long ice-green gown, elbow-length gloves and diamante earrings. Audrey got third. He saw her blink up at the sun and clench her lower lip in her teeth as all the contestants made a final circuit of the stage. The woggy-looking kid did a big cartwheel and everybody laughed and clapped.

'We were looking for something just a little bit different this year,' he heard the big judge say to the woman who looked like the mother of that kid.

Cunts. He didn't care about their stupid little show. He'd just get his daughter and piss off.

She came towards him, her cheeks splotched with red paint which matched the stain of heat rash bubbling on one leg.

He held out his arms. 'Third's not so bad, baby,' he said consolingly, stroking the shiny white sash.

'No good!' She struggled out of the satin coil and threw it on the ground. 'No good!' The ballerina slippers, scuffed and dirty, left grassy smudges on the sash. 'I wanta go home! I hate it here! Where's Mum? I wanta go home!'

'Yeah, okay, let's get outta here.' He'd seen one of the mothers raise her eyebrows at another.

The wind had come up; it was going to be a grey squally night. As they crossed the grass to the car, he remembered the business card dog-eared, grease-stained, at the back of his wallet. Worth a try.

'Hi, is Baz there?' he asked, when he rang the number on his mobile.

'Who's this?' asked a young male voice.

'Just tell him Bryon rang.' He suddenly felt really tired.

Audrey ran ahead, her tantrum forgotten, trying to do a cartwheel and giggling when she fell in a heap.

'You want to play, baby? You want to go on the swings?'

'Change, Dad.' She held up her arms. 'I'm cold.'

He helped her pull on the striped leggings and dark jumper that she chose. He managed to clumsily twist her hair into a flowered band to make a ponytail.

'Now we go home, Dad?'

'Not yet, kitten. We're going to take Uncle VisaCard and find a nice place to stay and watch telly and have all kinds of nice things to eat.'

'DVDs, Dad?'

'Yeah, DVDs.'

By the time they went to the only DVD place in town, chose *Harry Potter*, found out where the caravan park was, ordered a pizza and booked a cabin, night had come down. A dog raised its leg nonchalantly against the base of one of the old trees which spread their giant arcs over the street and a streetlight glinted off the statue of some long-dead pioneer as the dented Ford nosed its way up the hill. The faces at the windows of the Continental Hotel were fleshy slats against yellow glass, glimpsed through slim-line blinds which were new since the night he'd heard the liquid chimes of the clock striking midnight while the girl's breath sobbed beneath him.

The phone went off and he grabbed it up. He'd shoot the shit with Baz, talk about old times, ask how the business was, tell him yeah, he was still at the timber yard but he was assistant manager now.

'I don't know where you are,' the voice said, 'but when you get back I'll have your access rights revoked.'

'Fuck off!' The button on the phone killed her voice; he wished that it would kill her too.

As he unlocked the cabin door, he had the idea of turning the car round and driving and driving until he reached a place where white veils of heat drifted across the road and his eyelids were fattened by the sun.

He put the pizza box down on the table and went out to get his daughter. 'Wakey, wakey, sweetheart.' He carried her in, then wiped her face with a towel. He expected her to be whiny and querulous after her nap but she was quite composed. For dessert he'd bought a carton of strawberry ice cream and he watched her spoon it up carefully from the utilitarian white bowl.

'This has been a nice day,' she remarked conversationally, dabbing a tissue to her lips.

'Has it, Princess? Has it?'

'Yes. A nice day.' Then, frowning slightly, as though the memory cost her effort and she had to find her way back to it: 'Are we going to see Mum tomorrow?'

'Yes.' He tamped down the lid of the carton firmly and stowed it in the fridge.

'And then you're coming back home with Mum and me?'

He opened his mouth to form some easy assurance but perhaps it was her searchlight gaze or the gratitude he felt for 'nice day'. Maybe it would never get any better than this for him, or for her. (Helen would keep the trophies dusted, he knew that.) Whatever the reason, he felt he owed her something real. 'No,' he said. 'Probably not.'

'But you'll come and visit?'

'Yes.'

'Good.' She kept eating, calmly enough, then put down her spoon and neatly wiped her mouth. 'Can I go on the swings now?'

'You don't think you'll be sick?' he teased.

'No.' She looked at him patiently, already a small survivor, a sturdy castaway from a shipwreck of adult life. Audrey: it was a funny, old-fashioned name to give a kid.

He took her hand and together they trudged through the dark to the sandpit in the far corner of the caravan park. In the orb of torchlight, balanced on the metal seat, with her hair tucked under a woolly hat, she looked like an ordinary little girl.

'Harder, Dad, harder!'

Her face flew out of focus then came back to him; as he held the light on her, her features smeared with joy. Back in the cabin, he'd wanted to say that he'd always be there, that he'd do anything for her, anything, but his nerve had failed. Promises were a bit like beauty: illusory, subject to change. As he pushed his daughter higher, he had a sudden image of how he must appear, a dark figure looming at the edge of the wind, a form present but insubstantial, a white glare of face caught up in the crescendo of her happy scream:

'You're a ghost, Daddy! You're a ghost!'

Lust

They were driving back from town one afternoon, the mother and the daughter, driving back to the farm. It had been school speech day and the girl had cleaned up, as usual. She had walked up onto the stage half a dozen times while her mother watched from the end of a row of steel-framed, canvas-backed chairs. There was a stack of gilt-edged certificates on the girl's lap waiting to be pasted into the big white book at home. It was a warm day in early spring; the sky was shot through with trailing pieces of flotsam and hawthorn trees clouded the air with heavy scent.

'Did you know Florence had a baby when she was seventeen?' asked her mother.

'Had a baby,' repeated the girl stupidly. Her mind had been on tomorrow's German class. 'Had a baby.' She knew what having a baby meant. The girls who went off into the dark at the 50–50 dances at the local hall sometimes had a baby. The next dance those girls went to was their own, a shower tea before they started to show too much. Then the quick wedding in the dress with generous skirt panels and every tongue in the district wagging. That was what having a baby was about.

'She had a baby at seventeen,' said her mother. 'Nobody knew anything about it until it was happening.'

'Someone must have known,' said the girl. She imagined the swollen belly, the greyish-blue veins with their heavy cargo forking and tapering down to the dead end roads of capillaries. 'Someone must have known.'

Her mother pressed her lips together; tiny runnels of puce-coloured oil formed at the corners of her mouth. 'No one knew about it. There was a man who used to come around to do gardening... I don't know... he could have been having her for years, I suppose.'

Having…*haben*. The girl closed her eyes and began the declension. '*Ich habe, du hast, er sie es hat…*' She was studying German at school with two other girls. It was a small country high school made from blocks of grey stone, and languages were not given high priority. The girls who stayed on, who didn't leave to work as secretaries and nursing aides, took accounting and business mathematics. Every week the papers arrived from the correspondence school in Melbourne and the three 'Krauts', as they were known, found an empty classroom and sat down with their books and the Cassells dictionary to work it out for themselves.

'So…what happened?'

'It was taken away,' said her mother, turning the car off the road to begin the half-mile journey to the house. 'It was taken away and she never saw it again.'

'You must have been young, then.'

'I was ten,' said her mother. 'No one ever said anything to me. But I knew.'

'Your parents never said anything?'

'Nothing,' said her mother.

The girl felt the car jolt over the metal struts of the cattle pit, then settle into the familiar cushioning of mud. Her father was strip grazing beef cattle in the front paddock and slack-uddered Aberdeen Angus wandered across the track, black teats slapping between their flanks. One stopped in front of the car, trailed by a white-faced calf, which drooled milky saliva.

'Come on, scrubber.' The mother hit the horn. 'Out of the way!'

The cow put its head down, let out a moist half-bellow, then lumbered off.

'They're stupid bloody things,' said the girl.

'Language,' said her mother, pulling the car up in front of the house. 'Watch your language, please.'

'I look at it constantly,' said the girl, opening the door. 'G'day, spud face.'

Her brother, already home from the primary school down the road, was starting the evening chores. He was not good at school and was not expected to remain there after the day he turned fifteen. He would come home and help out on the farm and perhaps do a short course at the local ag. college later on. 'Good thing it's him and not Louisa,' the girl's father had said jokingly one evening. Girls were useless on the farm. The girl was expected to finish school and go on to teacher's college or even university and bring honour and achievement to her family by becoming an English teacher. She was her parents' offering to the people who lived in town and only worked five days a week.

She was usually excused from doing chores and this is why she pulled a face when her mother said, 'Dad needs you to shift the electric fence. Just move it ten yards towards the end of the paddock so the cows can get some new feed.'

'Can't he do it?' The girl indicated her brother.

'*He's* got enough to do. *He's* got to feed the calves. Now go on! It won't take a minute.'

The girl went into the washhouse, took her gumboots from beside the pile of old newspapers and went out, slamming the door on the way. 'Here, Pedro,' she called, and the dog, which looked like a big grey fox with black ears, grinned and ran alongside.

The girl's father owned a record of Richard Tauber singing 'Pedro the Fisherman' and, even when he was a pup, you couldn't keep the dog away from water.

The cows had chopped the paddock to muddy slush; her boots made faint sucking sounds as she pulled them out of watery, hoof-shaped craters stained gelatinously green and purple. A big arc of ibis whirred overhead, their wings calligraphy against a vast, silvery sky hung with ragged flags of cloud. 'More bloody rain,' thought the girl. She wondered if there was a place where rain was not a constant preoccupation – '…good lotta rain we've been havin', let's hope it holds up for the spring…' – and if this place existed, how a person got there.

The mud dragged at her heels and she could hear the wind's faint grey singing through the pine trees and see the reluctant sun gleaming on the strand of wire ahead. Next to it sat the metal box, the blunt heart which powered the current. The cows had stopped grazing and were following the dog, who trotted ahead, ears back, tail whisking the air.

'Garn, Pedro,' said the girl suddenly. 'Garn,' and the dog rushed barking at the nearest cow, and left a circlet of blood around the dark flank.

'Look at me, look at me,' he yipped to the girl. 'I'm a good dog, I'm a good dog,' and, elated with himself, rushed forward.

The girl felt the hard snout under her arm as she fell against the wire, felt the blue shard of light enter her skin and travel her arm to some distant citadel of bone. There was a moment of flying, a second suspended from time and then she lay sprawled back in the mud with the first soft slivers of rain pocking her face. A thread of steel stretched in her head, a fine singing cable which ran from fingers to scalp. The dog had lost all interest and stood immersed to his hocks in a small pewter-coloured lake, the water so still there were two dogs, dark grey muzzle to dark grey muzzle. The girl lay against the soft, sucking earth, feeling the rain on her face then pushed herself to her feet with legs shaky as a newborn calf's. She switched off the generator and trudged along the fence line, methodically pulling up the metal pegs and carrying them across the paddock to stake out the new strip of grass. The wire was completely harmless now, just a dead string of metal; nevertheless, her hand trembled when she touched it. On her way back to the house, she kept prodding at the flesh pierced by the current and felt a dull, echoing ache of pain.

'It bit me,' she said, coming into the kitchen. She held up her hand. 'The fence bit me.'

'They do that sometimes.' Her father set down the pink, gold-embossed teapot which had been a wedding present from one of his wife's cousins. There was a neatly split scone on the plate before him and a small, dainty glass dish held wedges of fruit cake. He did this every afternoon, came in for a cuppa, before he started the evening milking.

The girl's mother stood at the sink, hands swaddled in red and white gingham. 'You'll live,' she said to the girl. 'A few of those and you hardly notice them after a while.'

'In fact…' the girl's father spread butter on the edge of his scone '… you sometimes get cows that get immune to the pain, who don't take any notice of the fence at all. Just crash through. They're a nuisance,' he remarked, thoughtfully chewing. 'Yeah, they're a real nuisance.'

'Have we ever had any like that?' The girl sat down and helped herself to the teapot. It was near the end and liquid came out lukewarm and brackish.

Her father leaned back in his chair. 'I remember there was one old Friesian scrubber we had about the time you were born…'

'Oh, stop it. Louisa doesn't want to hear about that! Load of old rubbish!'

'She might be interested.' The girl's father tried for a grin.

'Don't be stupid!'

'I know who's stupid…'

'Shut up!' The girl set down her cup and felt the vibration retrace the path of the current. 'Just shut up!'

They shut up. They were not a family who talked much. The mother finished the dishes and the father finished his afternoon tea and together they went out to battle the mud. The girl cleared away the dirty plate and the teapot and then spread out her books on the end of the kitchen table. She kept thinking about Florence, who lived up north with her husband near the state border. They ran a small beef property and kept an orchard; there were cousins, older than the girl, who she had met once or twice. She remembered a childhood visit, her auntie wearing a soft flowered dress bending to kiss her, light twisting its way through avenues of peach and pear trees.

'It must have been awful for her,' she said, later that evening, as she smoothed down the plastic overlay which held the certificates in the big, white book.

'What?' The girl's mother was ironing up the other end of the table. There was no ironing board; she made do with an old blanket, folded in four, over which she placed an old tablecloth too old and frayed to be used for its original purpose. She hung up the girl's school dress and reached into the clothes basket for a handful of hankies.

'Florence. It must have been awful for her.'

Her mother adjusted the dial on the iron and licked the end of her index finger. There was a slight spitting sound as flesh touched hot metal. She started on the first of the handkerchiefs and the air filled with the smell of freshly laundered cotton and the soft 'thunk, thunk' of the iron.

'Lust. That's what she said it was. Lust. No one ever knew anything about it. Are you sure you want to wear that dress tomorrow? It's still cold in the mornings.'

'It's third term,' said the girl. 'It'll be all right.'

When she set off for school the next morning, the sky was dark pink, silhouetting the row of pines on the hill behind the house and leaking a reddish sheen of light across the paddocks. There had been a slight frost; the chill went straight through the dress and wrapped icy bands around the girl's legs. She didn't care. Anything was better than the ugly, box-pleated tunic which flapped and bagged around her knees. She stood at the side of the road, shivering, until the bus came around the corner. Once on board, the girl chose her seat carefully, not so far down the back that she would have to talk to the ratbaggy kids who shouted and threw paper and not so far up the front that these same kids would think she was stuck up and call her a dickhead. Years ago, as a shy young first former, she had been the subject of a lot of teasing and had learned the hard way. She was usually pretty friendly to everyone, even to Marlene Noonan, who always sat by herself, who had head lice and a father who interfered with her.

The girl spread her folder and the English–German dictionary across her knees and began the translation – *Morgenwind ungeflugelt/ Die beschattete Bucht/ Und im bespiegelt/ Sich die reifende Frucht...* – while the bus nosed along the back roads picking up kids for the high school, the tech school and the Catholic schools, before turning onto the highway and heading towards the town.

The morning had opened up to a thin blue sky with a dull scribble of mauve cloud low on the horizon. Cows grazed placidly in neat paddocks, motionless except for champing jaws and switching tails. 'Stupid bloody things,' thought the girl. As the bus drove up to the high school, she saw Aileen Morrow waiting, with the books and correspondence papers under her arm.

'G'day.'

'G'day. Look at that moll, will you.' Aileen indicated Susy Kane, who stood on the footpath, shouting something up at two Marist Brothers boys.

'What you need is a great big tool…' one of them yelled out the window, but the rest was drowned out by the bus pulling away.

'Yeah, I know. Slag,' said the girl, looking at the tunic hem banging against Susy Kane's thighs. 'Did you find a room?'

'Room Eight… and I scrounged a staffroom heater from Macca. That's a shitload of books you've got there.'

'I've got music after school,' said the girl defensively. She knew that people considered the weekly piano lesson strange, that they didn't understand that the black slotted notes flowed off the page to make a language of their own.

'Sooner you than me.'

Aileen Morrow's mother had been a red-haired Catholic girl from a farm north of the town, which meant that Bill Morrow had had to 'turn' when she married her. 'He married a Catholic and he had to turn.' That was how the girl's mother put it. (For years to come, the girl would imagine the religious conversion process as a series of steps sharply executed at right angles to each other.) Anyway, the local talk was that Bill Morrow had driven a hard bargain with the priests and that was why Aileen wasn't at the convent school across town. It set her apart in some ways; she ran with a bunch of wild girls from the little coastal town twenty miles away and was one of the students who went to sit with Father O'Donnell when he paid the school his annual visit.

'Where's Jenny?'

'Dunno. Crook, I think.'

'At least she doesn't have to go far for help.'

'Yeah, Daddy will make her better,' and their laughter was an acrid witches brew for Jenny Barlow, the doctor's daughter, a natural blonde who captained the netball team.

Jenny had round brown eyes and talked about becoming an air hostess if she failed her exams. 'If I fail…in November…' she'd say, gazing at them earnestly.

Failing in November was a constant preoccupation which united all three, cut off as they were from big-city facilities and without a proper teacher. The girl imagined it as a door at the end of a long corridor slamming slowly and inexorably shut.

'*Es schlug mein Herz. Gescwind zu Pferd.*' She spread out her books and began unravelling the sentences. Occasionally she glanced across at Aileen Morrow, who sat at the end of the table working silently on her own clumps of words.

'*Und fort, wild wie ein Held zur Schlacht./ Der Abend wiegte schon die Erde…*' The girl pushed back the radiator searing a cruel line of heat across her ankles.

'It's *der Pferd*, isn't it? *Der Pferd?* For horse?'

'*Das*,' said Aileen Morrow, sucking on the end of her pencil. '*Das Pferd*. Neuter. That horse was a gelding.'

'It wasn't hung like a horse?' asked the girl, and the two of them shrieked with laughter.

It made the girl look across at the pale brown freckles and the orange hair straggling out of its perished rubber band. People talked about Aileen, even though she didn't go into the park behind the school to meet boys at lunchtime. The girl remembered a story she'd heard from Elizabeth MacGuire, another Mick, about how a couple of years ago Aileen had invited Elizabeth and some other girls around to her place one Saturday afternoon when her parents were out.

'Can you do it?' Aileen Morrow had asked. 'Have you done it before?'

Mrs Morrow, returning home with a friend earlier than expected, had walked into a lounge room with the furniture pushed back against the wall and a circle of fourteen-year-old girls with their legs apart, masturbating. Word had got out; some mothers had forbidden their daughters to have anything to do with Aileen. She was considered bright but dangerous, a bad influence. 'Unstable' was how Elizabeth MacGuire's mother had put it. At the time, the girl had been agreeably scandalised, titillated, had half-wanted to have been there even though, out loud, she had mouthed the mothers' sentiments.

Now, as she looked across the graffiti-scarred table, she felt the need to offer something up. 'Did you know my Aunt Floss had a baby?' she asked Aileen Morrow.

'Yeah?' Aileen Morrow looked at her with eyes brown as stones in a shallow creek bed, eyes flecked with gold where the sun hit the water.

'She had a baby when she was seventeen. No one knew anything about it.'

'Someone must have known.' Aileen sucked on the end of her pencil. 'Someone must have known. What happened?'

'It was taken away from her and she never saw it again. Lust,' said the girl, thrusting doom into her voice and widening her eyes. 'Lust,' and the word arced across the room, a bright flying thing which burnt the away the hesitancy and nervous regard which had always existed between them.

'Lust,' groaned Aileen Morrow, throwing back her head and rocking to and fro on her chair. 'Oh, lust!' She flicked through the pages of the dictionary and struck a mock heroic attitude. *'Ich konnte vor Wollust sterben!'*

'Here, you silly moll,' giggled the girl. 'Let me have it,' and she bent over the dictionary, crooning, as her eyes rampaged down the columns of words.

'Ach, meine liebe Lustling, ich habe Lust im Morgen, *ich, habe…'*

'…Lust am Abend und Lust in der Nacht…' Aileen Morrow snatched the book back and pointed to the girl. *'Lustdirne. Du bist eine Lustdirne. Susy Kane ist eine grosse Lustdirne!'*

'*Lustdirne*! *Lustdirne*!' chanted the girl, banging her fists on the table. 'Here, give it here!

But Aileen Morrow held the book above her head. 'No.'

'Yes. C'mon, give us it!' The girl leapt and grabbed but Aileen Morrow caught the outstretched hand and pressed it onto the table, touching the tender place where the spark from the fence had lodged. The girl grunted then fell back, the table edge a hard ridge in the small of her back.

'Let go. It hurts.'

Aileen pressed a little harder. 'Does it hurt?' She said this in a quiet disinterested way, then shifted her weight and leaned over.

The girl smelt sweat and amber essential oil and a faint, musty note of menstrual blood.

'Does it hurt? How much?'

'Stop it.' The blood roared in the girl's head and there was a dark feeling gathering in her belly, like a dam about to break. She panted and flexed but it only made Aileen grin like a naughty little boy.

'Go on, make me.' She tightened her grip, released it, then tightened it again. 'Make me.'

'What's going on in here? What are you girls doing?'

Neither of them had heard the approach of Miss MacKenzie who stood in the doorway, watching and frowning.

'Fuck you!' hissed Aileen Morrow, then straightened and turned. 'Just playing, Miss MacKenzie.'

'Playing's for children. You'll never get to university at this rate, Aileen. Now tidy this place up before the bell goes.' She regarded them for a moment longer, then went out, sliding the door shut.

'You'll never get to uni if you break my heart,' sang Aileen Morrow under her breath as she bunched her orange hair into its rubber band and smoothed down her dress. 'Well, what are you looking at?'

But the staring girl couldn't have told her, even if she had held the words cupped in her hands. She stood there, feeling as though her limbs were bound by an invisible sheath, some warm sticky membrane which moulded and clung as she moved across the room.

'Good lesson?' asked her mother when she came to collect her that evening. She did this every Thursday, left the men of the family to do the milking while she drove into town to pick the girl up from music.

'OK.' The girl had sat in front of the baby grand and let her fingers move like sleepwalkers across the keys. She had listened to the tick-tick-tick of the metronome and watched her wavering reflection in the piano's black face while the teacher praised her sensitive phrasing. Now she sat in the car as the streetlights came on and stars pitted the indigo sky.

By the time they reached home, it would be dark. Her mother had switched on the heater and air warm as breath fanned the girl's neck and face, wafting old odours of dog hair and dust and the oily bottoms of potato chip packets towards her. She gagged and for a moment thought she would throw up but the feeling passed and she sat, dumbly breathing fetid air and watching the town give way to roads lined with dark trees. She pressed the soft place between thumb and forefinger on her left hand. She remembered the weight of Aileen Morrow's hips, the brown eyes above her flecked with gold, like light from the sunlit stones in a shallow creek bed.

'Did you ever tell Dad...tell Dad about Florence?'

'Yes.' Her mother's eyes didn't shift from the road. 'I told him when we decided to get married. It seemed the right thing to do.'

'And...what did he say?'

'He said...' Her mother accelerated towards a rabbit which dashed in front of the car but she missed it, missed it by a mile. 'He said that everyone was entitled to one mistake.'

Entitled. The girl closed her eyes and rolled the word around her tongue like a hard, green jewel. Entitled. It was like being given a prize. Or a curse.

'What if...what if she'd wanted to keep the baby...or hadn't found someone else...someone to marry?'

'What?' Her mother spoke in a slightly exasperated tone as she slowed the car then swung if off the road and over the cattle pit. 'That wouldn't have happened. It didn't happen.' She looked across at her daughter; in the dark her eyes gleamed flat and blank as still water. 'She turned out all right.'

'Yes.' The girl thought of the neat rows of peach and pear trees, the feel of flowered cotton over breasts. 'She did.' There was a constricted feeling in her chest and she felt she was suffocating, or drowning, being pulled beneath the blanket of hot air. She thought about her homework, about school tomorrow and the unfinished translation and dull rage filled her. 'Turn off the heater, will you?'

'We'll be there in a minute,' said her mother placidly. 'D'you want to freeze?'

'Yes.'

The girl wound down the window and thrust her head out. The wind was rising and carried the smell of water; by morning it would be raining again. She sucked down cold air, then blinked and stared and rubbed her eyes. She could make out dark shapes, moving, just beyond range of the headlights. For a moment, the girl thought the heat had affected her brain, that she was hallucinating the black boulders heaving up from the ground, but then she realised it was only the cows, coming towards her, out of the night.

The Snake Charmer

There were just the two of them on the hundred-acre spread that the drought had blasted to dust. The house was nothing flash, just a big ramshackle weatherboard crusted with scabs of paint; must give the old place a few coats, her father was always saying. Down the back was the orchard where she sometimes went to play, mounding the crumbling earth or dragging a twig through dirt. Once there had been peach and pear and apple trees and luxuriant strands of grapes but the drought had killed them all. The only tree left was the walnut and it hunched like an old man, branches straggling greyly towards the sun. Every year its fruit dropped to the ground and rotted into small black knots. Her father had told her never to eat them. They're old and no good and might poison you.

He had a job at one of the local factories – the farm didn't bring them in enough to live on – but if he was offered night shift he turned it down. Got to stay home and look after my little girl, and then he'd go on about how you couldn't be too careful, you couldn't trust anyone these days and that there were animals everywhere.

Every morning she stood on the veranda and watched his rust-streaked ute disappear in a brown cloud at the end of the track. Her mother had cleared out when she was born; it had been like this as long as she could remember. There was a framed photograph on the mantelpiece in the front room, dark eyes swimming up from the sepia – 'Lily' – and an indecipherable year scrawled across a laughing lipsticked mouth. She'd tried asking her father about it once but he'd just pursed his lips and turned away. You don't want to know about her was all he said.

He arranged for correspondence lessons because he didn't like her spending time in town. Mostly she stayed in the orchard, watching the wind press down the grass like an unseen hand, or wandered through the silent rooms, rummaging in drawers which held scraps of fabric and gold threads coiled like cries. There were odd sticks of furniture, shelves stacked with dull, cracked china and once she came across an old cupboard dangling a pink shred of silk. She stood in front of it, stroking and murmuring, then began jiggling the rusted lock. She didn't hear the ute outside or his footsteps behind her; she only felt the stinging blow to her head. It was the first time she'd seen him angry and, after that, she left the cupboard alone.

The summer she was twelve the sun burnt a white hole in the sky and lifted a blonde shimmer from the paddocks. The creek bed cracked into a thousand branching fissures and the snakes were everywhere. Bad year for snakes, people said to each other on the streets in town. They took to arming themselves with sticks and pieces of four-by-two when they went out because the snakes were seen slithering under houses and through the holes in shed floors. Out on the farm they coiled on dusty tracks made by cows as they walked in single file to nose at the brown sludge in the bottom of the troughs. She saw tails flick through grass and slide through caves of blackberry canes, dried brittle and white as bone, in the orchard. Every morning when she turned her face towards the fat yellow light streaming through the bedroom window, she saw them.

She lay in the pink room patterned with blue rabbits he'd painted when she was a little girl, touching her new hair and new flesh. The sun pierced her skin, streamed though her limbs then coiled in her belly like a heavy golden weight. She closed her eyes and saw sockets of gleaming ruby and scales streaming with light. She saw the snakes twisted in a solid, roiling mass around the base of the walnut tree. Don't go out there, her father said. He'd warned her about the snakes ever since she was a little girl. Sat her on his knee and told her how dangerous they were, how one bite could kill and that she should never trust them.

The summer they crawled out of the earth, he went around the house and jammed up all the holes while she set the table and put the kettle on to boil. Tea for them was never very much, just cold meat and bread and butter washed down by warm, brackish liquid. Afterwards they sat out on the veranda watching the sky stain crimson and the pale chip of moon ascend while he had a few beers and stroked the back of her neck. Getting to be a big girl now. She slid off his knee and went inside to the dishes then lay on the bed in the narrow pink room. She saw the fence posts around the orchard lean like drunk sentries; she saw the snakes, slicked with moonlight, gliding beneath the tree.

Night after night, she lay watching the moon swell while she waited for the sound of his snores. She'd tiptoe past his door then make for the empty rooms. There weren't any mirrors in the house and she'd stand staring at the darkened glass, trying to recognise the face she saw. She saw dark eyes and pale skin; she saw the faded cotton nightdress clustered with forget-me-nots and threaded with ribbon. She wanted to be beautiful; she wanted to wear pink silk. While the wind rattled the dead leaves in the orchard, she tugged and rattled the lock on the cupboard, willing the dry wood to splinters. Night after night she pounded the door and tore flesh from her fingers while the moon floated in its milky aureole, sheening the silk to membrane. The night it fisted into the sky as a bone-white bulge, she ran to the shed where he kept the old tools, snatched up a chisel and hacked and gouged at the lock. It gave way with a shriek and a moan and out they fell. The twisted satins and stained silks and jars of perfume and paint. The beads and finery and the jumble of dresses and shoes. 'Her things!' Lapis and flame-red, purple and gold. She held them against her, buried her face in them, stroked velvet and sequins and lace. Right at the bottom she found the white satin sheath, twisted, bloodied and torn. Ahhh. She saw it reflected in the window, radiant as an angel. Ahhh. She slipped it on, smoothing it over breasts and hips. Ahhh. She was in love. She smeared her eyelids with blue and slashed her lips with scarlet and drew circles of rouge on her cheeks.

She slopped her feet into high-heeled shoes and walked out into the night. Little puffs of dust rose up as she clopped along, following the moon to the orchard. It lay down a skin of blue light for her and under the tree she saw the snakes, heads rearing skyward and lidless eyes holding fractured silver. There were snakes with bellies stroked red with fire and black snakes patterned with diamonds. Snakes the colour of spring grass and snakes the colour of freshly turned earth. She stood before the harsh sibilant swaying, her limbs heavy and her blood thick as nectar. She couldn't get enough, but then they came towards her. They were all around her, a sea of hissing and when she saw they meant to have her, she ran. Jagged black sounds tore from her throat and she screamed that they would kill her, kill her as she fled through the orchard, tripping over gnarled tree roots and snagging a shoe. She kicked it free and loped clumsily along, clutching the sides of her dress. She was halfway across the paddock when she felt the first coldness coil around her ankle and slither up her calf. They were all over her as she twisted and stamped, all over her until she became a writhing column of scales. White satin shawled around her feet as she screamed and whimpered Daddy, Daddy. The sky tilted and she fell.

When she came to, her father was standing over her, holding the soiled dress. There was a white line above his lip and spittle showered her when he spoke. 'Do you know whose this was? This was your mother's! That whore! That cunt! This was what she wore the night of our wedding!' and then on and on, ranting, about that night – 'She laughed at me! wouldn't do what I wanted!' – and how she'd packed her bags and gone into town. Gone to the pub with the worst reputation and got work there. 'A barmaid! That whore! Stayed there in one of the rooms above, while half the town came and went!' On and on about the men he'd seen her with and the graffiti on the toilet doors: 'Want a root, ring Lily. Nine-Times-A-Nite-Lil-She's Allrite!' On and on about ruining his good name and all the time he was rubbing the dress against his trousers and twisting it in big knobbly hands.

She lay gazing up while he shouted about the pregnancy – 'She walked around in town with her belly out in front! That slut! That filth! – and the tiles running red with blood. 'They found her in the bathroom with her legs apart and I picked you up and took you home! Even though I didn't know you were mine! And this is how you repay me! You whore! You slag! Like this!' Holding up the wetly stained dress and flinging it at her. 'You're just like your mother! You're just like her!'

She lay there, a big swollen doll with a gaudy face. When she pulled on the dress, she saw splashes of blood and dark stains on her thighs. She didn't know what to do. He pushed her into the ute and they drove home across the paddocks. When she looked into his face, she didn't know what to do. She wanted to kill him and she wanted to say she was sorry. She didn't know what to do.

She stopped eating. She stopped eating and her blood dried up and every day she sat at the window watching the wind press down the grass like an unseen hand. Eat something, princess, he pleaded. Eat something, with tears in his eyes. When she first started pushing plates away, he'd tried to make a joke of it, said she was making herself look like the models in the magazines. He put food on a fork and tried to baby her but she turned her face from his. The wind blew through the house and sifted loose grains of sand from the orchard. *Hunger. Hunger.* It ate up her flesh and burnt in her eyes like a flame. He brought special treats from town, tempted her with sticky drinks and pastries but she threw them on the floor. He'd shout at her, then beg for forgiveness and cry. Sometimes she'd watch his grovelling and tears and she'd smile.

They never spoke about that night but he smashed up the cupboard and made a bonfire from it and the clothes. I reckon she put a spell on you, he said, as the flames crisped velvet and silk. Red light streaked his face; red whispers filled her ears and wrapped around arms and legs withering to sticks.

At night she lay on the bed in her shrinking tent of skin while strange beasts and horned dragons roared above. Her eyes filled with dark islands and her ears with the sound of flames. Armies of grasshoppers rampaged across the earth, stripping the grey paddocks bare. *Hunger. Hunger.*

He put a new fence around the orchard but needn't have bothered; the snakes had gone. Disappeared into the cracked earth or the heat which hung like a fiery miasma at the end of the track. Walking one morning under a bleached sky she found the fragile sheath sequined with scales and felt its sharded heat. You're a real snake charmer, dead set, he said, when she brought it home and laid it on the dressing table in her room. He put out his hand shyly but she turned away. She lay on the bed, folded hands white as wafers, listening to the click, click, click of the grasshoppers.

She imagined the hard shiny bodies; she imagined her own as a fragile sheath brittle as spun glass and translucent as fire. Day after day she grew lighter until her breath barely took up room in the world. *Hunger. Hunger.* She closed her eyes and saw walls of flame sweeping the land. She heard the wind blow through her skin and rattle it like a husk.

Love Letters In the Sand

I used to drive down the coast just to sleep with her. At three a.m. the only light that pocked the slopes of the final switchback that slid into town was the chill glare of insomniac TV. The light she left on over the back porch was a red-cellophaned bulb, a smouldering ember on that street where the only sounds came from the Koori house on the corner, that reggae beat blood-heavy as a club. A half-tab of speed would fire me past Kempsey, where I'd scald my hands on truck-stop coffee, ignoring the *are you a woman or a man?* just to reach her before dawn.

That harsh iodine breeze slammed all the doors in that place where the bare boards gaped like ribs and lilac tangled the fence. She'd stumble to the door, laughing sleepily, saying she'd been in bed with Johnny, the tarry taste of second-hand alcohol in my mouth then grazing her nipples but she always wanted the beach first, would clamour for the ocean with its frill of foam and flat stones. Beneath the patina of anorexic light, my flannelette shirt snagged her to me because she'd only ever wear a singlet and those faggy satin boxer shorts. Always the heart-flaming sprint along the sand then giggling, falling into each other, shedding clothes and stumbling to the water. Her body rising naked from the sea was a baptism, a new life that I entered as she arched against the palm tree, straining to take my whole hand, her eyes darkening, widening as the rough bark inscribed her flesh.

Afterwards we'd pick up driftwood and write dumb things in the sand, the way kids or teenagers do: LISA LOVES GLENN THIS IS TRUE TRUE LOVE NEVER DIES, then the walk back, passing the half-bottle of Johnny companionably while the old guys returning home from a night's fishing offered a wavering salute. I'd whistle some corny tune *and when you smile the world is brighter / you touch my hand and I'm a king* while she told me stories about her father the truck driver, Daddy's girl, Daddy's little princess but nothing weird, no funny business. Her mother was one of those country women who get broken fairly early, a farm girl knocked up at seventeen but pretty, with that black Irish hair and big grey eyes, runner-up in Miss Taree Showgirl one year. *I used to think I owned the world, sitting up beside him in that cabin.*

When we first got together, I tried to impress her with stories of Venice, Paris, the names running together like a string of pearls, but she was never interested. *You know too much.* Frowning. She liked to lie in bed planning her wedding, where the bridesmaids wore tuxedoes and Elvis was the best man but, apart from that, we didn't talk a lot. There was a whole rack of clothes in one wardrobe: linen shirts, pleated pants, silk camisoles hanging like shapely ghosts on padded hangers. She'd had an older lover who had wanted to set her up in style in Sydney but when I asked what went wrong all she said was *I got tired of being around all those fat-arsed old dykes who played golf and wondered what to do with their money.* She'd kept the ruby ring the woman gave her and the sapphire and diamond earrings, left them lying around on top of the wood veneer dressing table pushed into a corner of the room. In the day, she worked at the supermarket, avoiding the hands of the manager, who was always telling her she should model, and then there was me, telling her she should go back to school because she was getting too old to be anybody's pretty girl. She just used to stare and shrug. *I'll probably have a baby.*

There was a boy she saw sometimes who used to live across town — he could have been her brother except on him it was spindly, all angles and bones — and she talked about having a baby with him. *It would be easy*, she told the boy with his porn-page mind when he said he liked it three ways with chicks. That night, I raked her so hard I tore her, left her sobbing against the gaping chequerboard of tiles while I drove to the brick box on drought-patched lawn. I saw the wife gone to fat and the two grubby brats, the crushed plastic toys and crushed cans. That skinny little shit. I could have broken him in two. She was still there where I'd left her and I helped her clean up, spread the cuts with calendula *does it hurt, baby, does it hurt?* then lapped her tenderly as the sea lapped the small cove early that morning, walking though the opaque streets as dawn broke with the black men throwing empties *Garn, ya fucking lesos, ya both need a good root,* and the laughter of their women, jagged as glass, behind them. LISA & GLENN 4 EVER LISA LOVES GLENN THE BEST covering the shore with hearts and flowery scrolls the sea so far out it was a blue lisp at the horizon and the rising sun coming through the clouds like a Helen Steiner Rice greeting card.

She said she wasn't seeing him but weekends his smell was in the bed with the sand from our unwashed feet and the trails of lavender massage oil cut with the sharp scent of her cunt. She said *I'm not seeing him any more* but I heard her late at night giggling like a teenager into the phone. She told me she wasn't seeing him but I wasn't surprised about the limpet embedded in its shifting red-plush sea, hearing her gasp it out as I held her bent over the toilet, *he doesn't know, don't tell him.* That skinny little shit. I should have broken him in two.

I held her the next morning and the next while she moaned and retched and I was so glad she was suffering. *I can't do this on my own,* heaving and snivelling. *We could do it together* but she said the kid would get teased at school and she didn't want that. *What do you want? What do you?*

Not this! It feels like a leech inside of me! But she let one week go past then another while the thing swelled softly under her heart. She kept crying and moaning and I got scared she'd sit in a scald of water till the blood ran out, even though it didn't have to be that way; it wasn't like it was in my time, the late night call to a doctor who was a friend of someone your mother knew. *You must have been a beautiful cos baby look at you now...* Our faces smeared like ghosts in the fish and chip shop window, me whistling and clowning, the juice from fresh scallops pearling on our chins and the cracking gold batter blistering fingers and lips. *You don't have to say you love me*…uncorking the Moët, the bubbles pocking and bursting as I swilled them from my mouth to hers and we tossed the salt-stained paper into the bush then trawled sticks through the sand GARTH IS A BIG COCKSUCKER GARTH LIKES IT UP THE ARSE rocking with laughter, her belly already rounding and her breasts dropping into my hands like heavy fruit. I told her about the little stone statues, some no bigger than a thumb, dug up from European soil. The Venus of Willendorf, the Venus of Laussel… *Breast and bellies to feed the world.* I even showed her pictures in bed. *They're ugly. I don't want to look like them…they're ugly, ugly, ugly…*

We caught the train in the middle of the night, the Sitting Up All Night Train to the Big Smoke. A group of hippie feminists up the front of the carriage were loud with jolly anthems – they were still doing those things back then – but I could have told those girls in pink overalls it's not all vanilla pods and butterflies across the surface of the mind. She sat next to a farmer's wife who kept trying to make conversation about the love of Jesus. *He sees everything.* Yeah, he must have seen my Uncle Stan who wasn't my real uncle heavy as a bull on top of me. (He caught me with Chrissi McKenzie when I was fourteen and told me I needed straightening out.) Mummy didn't believe her prince was a rapist but she paid to have the child cut out of me and threw more money on the table. I left home the next morning and sold them what they wanted, a slender thing with light brown hair called Marni but I never put that money up my nose or up my arm. It was night school at the tech for eight years, the boys filling my test tubes with coloured water just to prove that chicks can't do science. (The day I left the parlour I cut off all my hair and let the dye grow out my pale ginger crop and freckles riding jeans and vest and Cuban-heeled boots.)

I found the places in the city we were allowed to be, dark caverns with leaky red light and watery, overpriced drinks and that's where I met Madelaine. Madelaine, the hyper-femme who later power-dressed, Madelaine smooth as a length of silk who liked it a bit rough and who paraded me before all those cross-your-legs look-the-other-way gay ladies who called themselves bachelor girls to the world and who gave dinner parties for each other on the weekends. *The Beethoven…so tense it was almost barbaric, darling…the Shostakovich…* (I didn't think they would want to hear about Johnny Cash or Jim Reeves.) Sunday afternoons women in pearls wine on the art gallery lawn light to be strolled through in Corot, Renoir and Degas. *Look at the brush strokes…* Madelaine taught me to see the smoky red and violent blues the peach-yellows and lucid-greens… *You've got a good eye, you could be good at this* but I never wanted long lunches with corporate sponsors or curatorial conferences with fag-hags and their petboys. A shattered cup doesn't care what you look like, the shards of porcelain cool under your fingers. When you heal a damaged painting, you pull on gloves as fine as fibre. You let your eyes caress, you let them wander until they find the fissure the fault the wound. I chose fractured beauty and became the best.

Miro, Seurat, Picasso. I flipped over pages thick as cream. A row of dreary sheep towns slipped through the neon-crenulated night that faded to a flayed big sky. *Weird, huh?* (I thought the Miro would make her laugh.) *You know too much*, drowsily, her head on my shoulder. *Your sister's such a sweet girl.*

The Christian woman nursed her basket of eggs and watched us lick the custardy ooze of vanilla slice from our fingers as the train lurched and clanked into Central. *Where are we going?* Like a child, an orphan carried along on the grey commuter fuzz, then I held her hand in the taxi against the sneer of the Lebanese driver and the downcast eyes of the Madonna dangling above the dash. It was just an ordinary house, white weatherboard with a dark green trim, and the Christian woman's sister opened the door. I signed the next-of-kin sheet, the name Miss Glenda Browne, glancing back indifferently as a stranger. Then I let her go, imagined her spread like a piece of meat as I stared around the waiting room with its earnest posters, the camomile paint hollowing the cheeks of the middle-aged woman with the wedding ring in the corner. When she saw me looking, she dried her eyes and told me I was being a good friend.

Friend: the word sounded sweet as baby pap. I was never anybody's friend, always the lover, the one who courted with perfume and silk, who flattered and flirted and opened doors and pulled out chairs. I loved the beautiful ritual like a slow and stately dance, but I never let any of them touch me, not once. GLENN AND LISA TOGETHER 4EVER TWO HEARTS BEAT AS ONE

When she came down the corridor thirty-three minutes later, she looked wobbly as a newborn calf but was staying on her feet. We took a cab to an expensive restaurant where we ate underdone rack of lamb and white chocolate mousse and afterwards I sipped coffee black as sorrow while she made spirals of sugar grains on the table. Our conversations were small bleeds against a September afternoon, the harsh spring light abrading her face and I suddenly saw her in ten years a small-town hausfrau holding court in the main street, where the topic was immigration or the latest third grade teacher. *Daddy's little girl, Daddy's little princess*, surrounded by women with crow eyes and cow ankles. We sat there and our words became islands and clots.

All the way back, we slept curled together like sticky children, fell into stale sheets and woke to find the stain seeping crimson against beige. We walked. The sea was iced, grey seagulls circled floating carrion and she battered a piece of flotsam through the sand.

I woke at five; the bed still held her heat but she was in the bathroom, just a tufted halo where the dark hair had been and her arms gleaming like a slaughterhouse. We wrestled for the razor, her mad breath rasping cunt bitch dyke, then into the lounge, the crystal vase trailing jasmine splintering into light. I cradled her as she sobbed and we lay together in crushed flowers and warm blood. I knew then she would never give up that white satin dream, the place in the bland clear light of day where lawnmowers snarled and I was stigmata. Blood coined on makeshift bandages. (I had the long cut stitched and it left a scar like a crescent moon.)

She watched me drive away and I didn't wave and she didn't wave but it seemed that I followed her in my mind for years, tracking endless possibilities: the strip club, the dot.com Businesswoman of the Year, the registry office marriage where she wore a burnt orange retro shift and he was lead guitarist of a famous rockabilly band, he was a solicitor with a five-bedroom quasi-Georgian solid brick home, he was a photograph face down on the bedside table while she wheeled out the garbage and promised the youngest a trip to *Surfers and other great places Mum used to go.*

That last walk on the beach as the kelp scrawled the waves with black weals, she wrote YOU KNOW TOO MUCH, the wet blurry coda ABOUT ME just a melting furrow, but always before my eyes as the tide sliced it away, a final disclaimer glimpsed then abandoned like debris, a piece of mangled road kill rotting and blackening to slush, drowning in its muck of glamour, a bog of memory slippery and elusive as the past.